FLORA'S FEAST

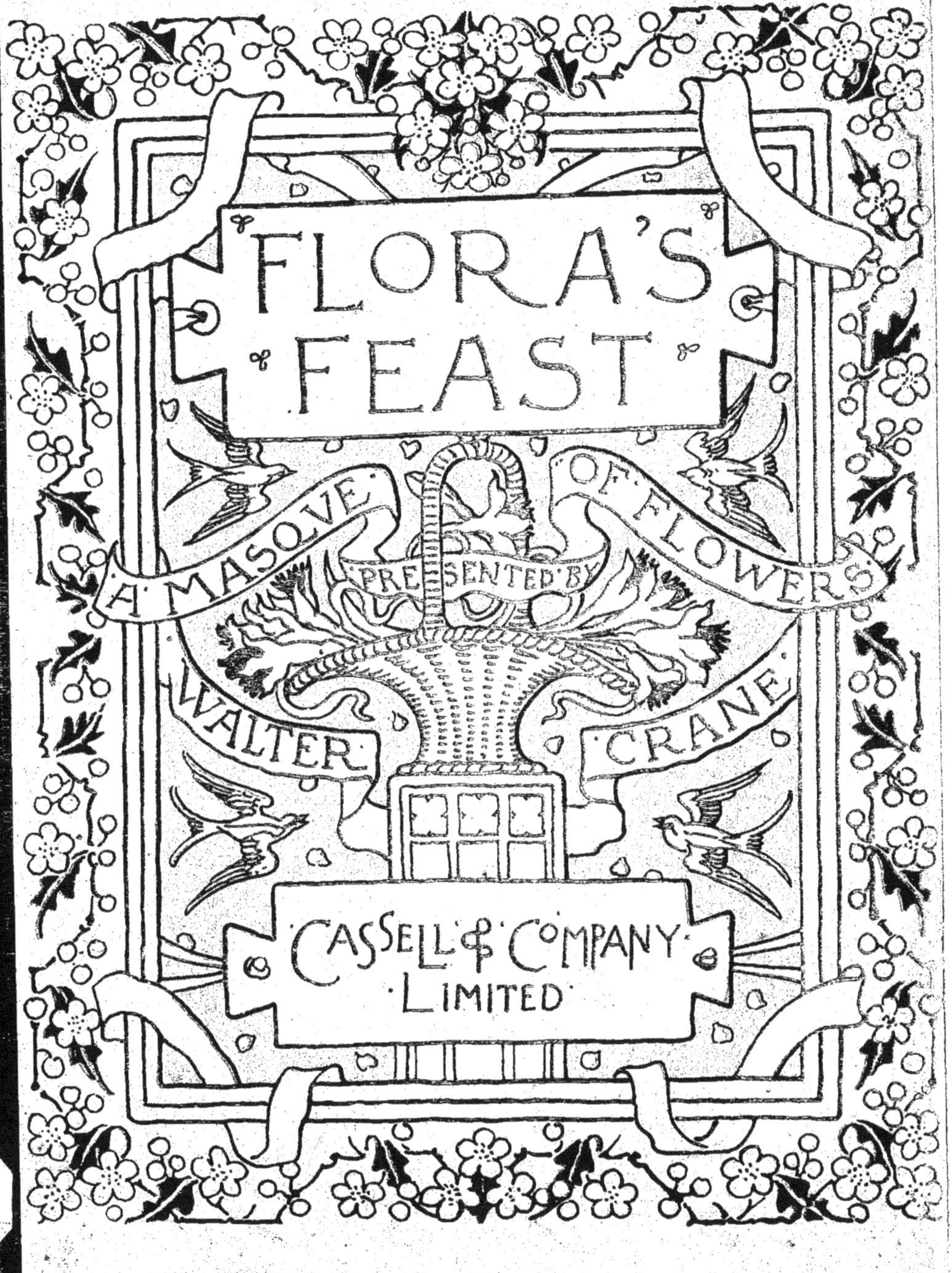

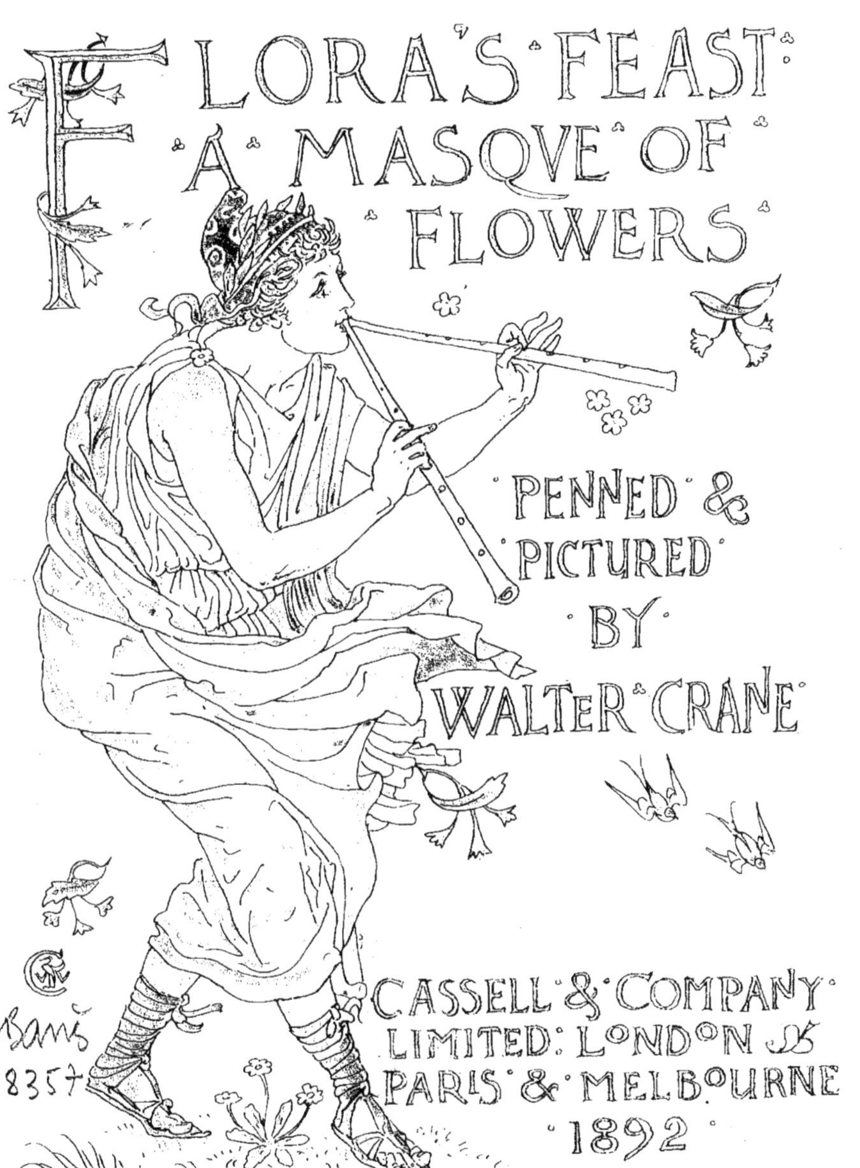

FLORA'S FEAST
A MASQVE OF
FLOWERS
PENNED &
PICTURED
BY
WALTER CRANE
CASSELL & COMPANY
LIMITED: LONDON
PARIS & MELBOURNE
1892

The sullen winter nearly spent,
Queen Flora to her garden went,
To call the flowers from their long sleep,
The year's glad festivals to keep:

And one by one each
making bold
Their silken vesture
to unfold,
And peeping forth to meet
the sun,
The long procession is begun:-

The Snowdrops first upon
the scene,
White-crested braved King
Frost's demesne:

The little Crocus
reaches up
To catch a sunbeam
in his cup.

The Daffodil his trumpet blows,
And after Spring a
hunting
goes.

Anemones rode out the gale,
Frail Wind-flowers flutter'd,
         red & pale:

The Violet, and the Primrose dame,
With modest mien but hearts
aflame,

Green-kirtled from the brooklet's fold,
The rustic maid Marsh- Marigold:

The "Lady smocks all silver white"
The milkmaids of the meadows bright,

There shining Buttercups abound,
Among the Cowslips on the
ground.

Here Lords and Ladies of the wood,
With shaking spear, and riding-
hood:

Black knight-at-arms, the white-
plumed Thorn;
In pomp the Crown-Imperial borne.

While Tulips lift the banner red,
Or fill the cups with
fire instead.

Sweet Hyacinths their bells did ring,
To swell the music of the Spring.

With blazoned pennons from each spear,

The Iris and the Flag ap- pear

Sweet masking May, in white or
                                red,
Her snowy cloud   of   blossom
                                    spread.

And Chaucer's Daisy small & sweet
"Si douce est la Margarete".

The little Lilies of the Vale,
White ladies delicate & pale;

Great Peonies in crimson pride,
And budding ones in green that hide:

Fair Columbines that drew the car

Of Venus

from her distant

star:

And Love's own flower the blushing Rose,
The Queen of all the garden close:

And Roses from the hedgerow wild,
Behind their thorns that faintly smiled.

And from the cressy brook's green side,
"Forget-me-not", a small voice cried.

Here stately Lilies, pale and proud,
In vesture pure as summer cloud;

Or, burning like an orange flame,
With torches borne aloft they came.

The Monk that wears the hood of blue,
The Bells of Canterbury, too:

Tide Oxeyes in the meads
that gaze

n scarlet Poppy-heads a-blaze:

re Evening Primrose
lights her lamp,
A beacon to the garden camp:

Then Lilies of the day are done,
And sunk the golden westering sun.

Fresh Pinks cast incense on the air,
In fluttering garments fringed & rare.

Their cousin from the corn in blue;
Corn Marigold of golden hue.

he fond Convolvulus still clings,
The Honeysuckle spreads his
wings.

The Hollyhock
his standard
high,
Bears proudly to
the autumn
sky.

The blazing Sunflower, black and
bold,
Burns yet to win
the sunset's
gold,

That, reddening on the Triton's
                        spear,
Foretells the waning of the year.

When lilies, turned to Tigers, blaze
Amid the garden's tangled maze.

There still in triumph, stiff with gold,
The rich Chrysanthemums unfold.

Ere doth the floral pageant close
  With one last flower –
      a Christmas Rose.

∞ The End. ∞

A *Classified Catalogue*

OF

CASSELL & COMPANY'S PUBLICATIONS.

1d.

Cassell's Penny Illustrated Stories. Consisting of a Series of New and Original Stories by Popular Authors. Fully Illustrated. Monthly. *(List sent free on application.)*

Historical Cartoons, Descriptive Account of.

Cassell's New Poetry Readers. Illustrated. 12 Books. Each. *(See also 1s. 6d.)*

Cassell's School Certificates. *(Also at 3d.)*

The Secret of Success and How to Attain it. By John W. Kirton, LL.D.

2d.

Cassell's New Standard Drawing Copies. 6 Books. Each. *(Also at 3d. and 4d.)*

Cassell's School Board Arithmetics.

Cassell's Modern School Copy Books. 12 Books. Each.

Cassell's Graduated Copy Books. 18 Books. Each.

The Polytechnic Building Construction Plates. A Series of 40 Drawings. 1½d. each.

How should Railway Fares be Charged? By R. McEwen.

3d.

CASSELL'S NATIONAL LIBRARY. Paper covers, 3d. each; cloth, 6d. *(A full List of the Volumes now ready sent post free on application.)*

Cassell's Readable Readers. Illustrated and strongly bound. Two Infant Readers at 2½d. and 3d., and Six Books for the Standards, at 6d. to 1s. 1d. Also a superior edition at 7d. to 1s. 3d. *(List on application.)*

Cassell's Standard Drawing Copies. 6 Books. Each. *(See also 2d. and 4d.)*

Cobden Club Pamphlets. *(List on application.)*

The True Unity. By the Ven. W. M. Sinclair, B.D.

4d.

Cassell's Standard Drawing Copies. 2 Books. Each. *(See also 2d. and 3d.)*

The Modern School Readers. Four Infant Readers at 3d. to 5d., and Six Books for the Standards at 7d. to 1s. 6d. *(A List on application.)*

The Modern Reading Sheets. In Three Series, each containing Twelve Sheets, 2s. each. *(See also 5s.)*

Readers for Infant Schools, Coloured. 3 Books. Each containing 48 pages, including 8 pages in Colours. Each.

Shakespeare's Plays. 36 Parts. Each.

Sheridan and Goldsmith's Plays. Separate. Each.

EDUCATIONAL.

6d.

Laundry Work (How to Teach It). By Mrs. E. Lord.

The Modern Geographical Readers.

Introductory Lessons. For Standard I. . . . . 6d.
Introductory Lessons. For Standard II. . . . . 8d.
England and Wales. For Standard III. . . . 10d.
Scotland, Ireland, British North America, Australasia. For Standard IV. . . . . 1s. 0d.
Europe. For Standard V. 1s. 0d.
The World. For Standards VI. and VII. . . . 1s. 8d.

Shakespeare's Plays for School Use. Cloth. Each. Richard III. Henry V. Hamlet. Julius Cæsar. Coriolanus. Richard II. King John. Merchant of Venice. Henry VIII.

Euclid, Cassell's First Four Books of. Paper, 6d. *(Cloth, 9d.)*

Drawing Books for Young Artists. Each.

How to Draw Elementary Forms, Models, &c.
How to Draw Floral and Ornamental Forms.
How to Draw Landscapes, Trees, Ships, &c.
How to Draw Animals, Birds, and Dogs.

Arithmetics, The Modern School. By George Ricks, B.Sc. In 7 Books. Stands. I. to IV., paper covers, 2d. each; cloth, 3d. each. Books for Stands. V. to VII., paper covers, 3d. each; cloth, 4d. each; Answers, 6d. Complete in One Vol., with Answers, 2s.

Cookery for Schools. By Lizzie Heritage.

Cassell's National Library. Vols., in cloth. *(List of Vols. post free on application.)*

MISCELLANEOUS.

How Intemperance has been Successfully Combated. By the Duchess of Rutland.

Uniform Imperial Postage. By Robert J. Beadon, M.A.

Shall we Know One Another in Heaven? By the Rt. Rev. J. C. Ryle, M.A., Bishop of Liverpool.

Reunion among Christians. By the Rev. Reginald Smith.

Cobden Club Pamphlets. *(List on application.)*

Local and Centralised Government in Ireland. By W. F. Bailey.

Imperial Federation. Report of the Conference.

Appreciation of Gold. By William Fowler, LL.B.

6d.
cont'd.

CASSELL'S PICTURE STORY BOOKS.

Each containing Sixty Pages of Pictures, Stories, &c.

Little Talks. | Little Chimes. | Auntie's Stories.
Bright Stars. | Daisy's Story Book. | Birdie's Story
Nursery Joys. | Dot's Story Book. | Book.
Pet's Posy. | A Nest of Stories. | A Sheaf of Tales.
Tiny Tales. | Good-Night Stories. | Dewdrop Stories.
Chats for Small Chatterers.

SIXPENNY STORY BOOKS.

The Smuggler's Cave. — Little Lizzie. — Little Bird. — Luke Barnicott.—Little Pickles.—The Elchester College Boys.— —The Delft Jug.—My First Cruise.—The Little Peacemaker.—The Boat Club.

7d.

Cassell's "High School" Readers. Illustrated and strongly bound. Six books at 7d. to 1s. 3d.

9d.

Things New and Old; or, Stories from English History. By H. O. Arnold-Forster, M.P. Fully Illustrated. Strongly bound in Cloth. Standards I. and II., 9d. each. Standard III., 1s. Standard IV., 1s. 3d. Standards V., VI. and VII., 1s. 6d. each.

10d.

Cassell's Historical Readers.
Stories for Children from English History. Standard 3, 10d.
The Simple Outline of English History. Standard 4, 1s.
The History of England for Elementary Schools. Standards 5, 6, 7, 2s. *(See also 1s. and 2s. For UPPER STANDARDS.)*
Part I. From the Earliest Times to Elizabeth. 1s.
Part II. From Elizabeth to Modern Times. 1s.

1/-

THE WORLD'S WORKERS.

New and Original Volumes by Popular Authors. With Portraits. *(See also 3s.)*

John Cassell.
Charles Haddon Spurgeon.
Dr Arnold of Rugby.
The Earl of Shaftesbury.
Sarah Robinson, Agnes Weston, & Mrs. Meredith.
Mary Carpenter and Mrs. Somerville.
Thomas A. Edison & Samuel F. B. Morse. By Dr. Denslow and J. Marsh Parker.
Charles Dickens. [Moore.
Sir Titus Salt and George
Florence Nightingale, Catherine Marsh, Frances Ridley Havergal, Mrs. Ranyard ("L.N.R.").
General Gordon.
Dr. Guthrie, Father Mathew, Elihu Burritt, Joseph Livesey.
Abraham Lincoln.
Sir Henry Havelock and Colin Campbell, Lord Clyde.
David Livingstone.
George Müller and Andrew Reed.
Richard Cobden.
Handel.
Turner the Artist. [son.
George and Robert Stephenson.
Benjamin Franklin.

SHILLING STORY BOOKS. All Illustrated, cloth gilt.

Bunty and the Boys.
The Heir of Elmdale.
The Mystery at Shoncliff School.
Claimed at Last, and Roy's Reward.
Thorns and Tangles.
The Cuckoo in the Robin's Nest.
John's Mistake.
The History of Five Little Pitchers who had very Large Ears.
Diamonds in the Sand.
Surly Bob.
The Giant's Cradle.
Shag and Doll, and other Stories.
Aunt Lucia's Locket.
Among the Redskins.
The Ferryman of Brill.
Harry Maxwell.
The Magic Mirror.
The Cost of Revenge.
Clever Frank.
A Banished Monarch.
Seventeen Cats.

"LITTLE FOLKS" PAINTING BOOKS.

Each containing Outline Illustrations for Painting on nearly every page.
"Little Folks" New Painting Book. | "Little Folks" Illuminating Book.
A Book of Fruits and Blossoms for "Little Folks" to Paint.

ILLUSTRATED BOOKS FOR THE LITTLE ONES.

Containing interesting Stories, with Full-page Illustrations. In handsome Picture Boards. *(Also cloth gilt, 1s. 6d.)*

Tales Told for Sunday.
Sunday Stories for Small People. [Sunday.
Stories and Pictures for
Bible Pictures for Boys and Girls.
Firelight Stories.
Sunlight and Shade.
Rub a-dub Tales.
Fine Feathers and Fluffy Fur.
Scrambles and Scrapes.
Tittle Tattle Tales.
Wandering Ways.
Dumb Friends.
Up and Down the Garden.
All Sorts of Adventures.
Some Farm Friends.
Those Golden Sands.
Our Sunday Stories.
Our Holiday Hours.
Indoors and Out.
Little Mothers and their Children.
Our Schoolday Hours.
Creatures Tame.
Our Pretty Pets.
Creatures Wild.

EDUCATIONAL.

Cassell's Map-Building Series. By H. O. Arnold-Forster, M.P. Per Set of 12.

Hand-and-Eye Training Cards for Class Use. By George Ricks. In 5 Sets. Each.

Latin Primer, The First. By Prof. Postgate, M.A.

Science Applied to Work. By J. A. Bower. Illustrated.

Science of Everyday Life. By J. A. Bower. Illustrated.

Reckoning, Anglo-American Art of. By C. Frusher-Howard. *(See also 2s. and 5s.)*

Cassell's "Modern School" Test Cards. Seven Sets of 40 Cards in Case. Each.

Cassell's "Combination" Test Cards. Six Sets of 36 Cards with Answers, in Packet. Each.

Flowers, Studies in. In Thirteen Packets, each containing Six Flowers. Each Packet.

History, The Simple Outlines of. Illustrated.

Complete Tot Book for all Public Examinations.

Spelling, Morell's Complete Manual of.

1/- cont'd.

Euclid, Cassell's. First Six Books, with the 11th and 12th of Euclid.
Drawing Copies, Cassell's Modern School. First Grade —Freehand. (*Also Second Grade, free hand,* 2s.)
German Reading, First Lessons in. By A. Jägst.
Cassell's Historical Course for Schools.
  1. Stories from English History, 1s.
  2. The Simple Outline of English History. 1s. 3d.
  3. The Class History of England. 2s. 6d.
Carpentry Workshop Practice, Forty Lessons in. Polytechnic Technical Scales. Set of 10 in cloth case. (*See also* 10s. 6d.)
Cassell's Miniature Library of the Poets. In Two Vols. Half cloth. Each. (*See also* 2s. 6d.)

MISCELLANEOUS.

The Letters of "Vetus" on the Administration of the War Office.
A Shilling's-Worth of All Sorts.
Chips by an Old Chum; or, Australia in the Fifties.
Souvenir of Ravenswood. At the Lyceum Theatre. Illustrated.
An Address in School Hygiene. By Clement Dukes, M.D.
A Handbook to London in English and French.
Souvenir of the Dead Heart. By Watts Philips. Presented at the Lyceum Theatre, by Henry Irving. Illustrated.
Bits and Bearing-Reins, and Horses and Harness. By E. F. Flower.
Circulation or Stagnation. By Sir E. Chadwick, K.C.B.
The Old Fairy Tales. With Illustrations. (*Also at* 1s. 6d.)
Potato Culture and Disease Prevention. Illustrated.
Lawful Wedlock; or, How Shall I Make Sure of a Legal Marriage? By Two Barristers.
Advice to Women on the Care of their Health, before, during, and after Confinement. By Florence Stacpoole.
Our Sick and How to Take Care of Them; or, Plain Teaching on Sick Nursing at Home. By Florence Stacpoole.
Born a King. By Frances and Mary Arnold-Forster. Illustrated.
London Charities (Unendowed). By Robert Chignell.
Life in our Villages. Letters of the Special Commissioner of the *Daily News.* (*Also in cloth,* 2s.)
All About the Royal Navy. By W. Laird Clowes. Illustrated.
Our Home Army. By H. O. Arnold-Forster, M.P.
Four Years in Parliament with Hard Labour. By C. W. Radcliffe Cooke, M.P. *Third Edition.*
A Minimum Wage. By Alfred Morris. A new Novel dealing with Present-Day Social Questions.
Local Option in Norway. By Thomas M. Wilson, C.E.
International Fishery Disputes. By T. H. Haynes.
The Dwellings of the Poor. Report of the Mansion House Council. 1892. Illustrated.
The Housing of the Poor. By F. H. Millington.
Town Holdings. 1890. Digest. Vol. III.
British Difficulties under Solution. By F. R. Hungerford.
In a Conning Tower. By H. O. Arnold-Forster, M.P. Illustrated.
A Manual of Political Questions of the Day. By Sydney Buxton, M.P. Paper covers. (*Also in cloth,* 1s. 6d.)
Yule Tide: Cassell's Christmas Annual.
Skin, The Health of the. By E. B. Shuldham, M.D.
The Sugar Convention. By the Rt. Hon. Lord Farrer.
Free Trade in Sugar. A Reply to the Right Hon. Lord Farrer, by George Martineau.
Pre-Raphaelites, The Italian, in the National Gallery. By Cosmo Monkhouse. Illustrated.
Local Government in England and Germany. By the Rt. Hon. Sir Robert Morier, G.C.B., &c.
Irish Parliament, The, from 1782 to 1800.
Irish Union, The: Before and After. By A. K. Connell, M.A. *Cheap Edition.* (*Also in cloth,* 2s. 6d.)
How to Select Spectacles. By Dr. C. Bell Taylor.
Practical Kennel Guide. By Dr. Gordon Stables.
Cookery, Cassell's Shilling.
Choice Dishes at Small Cost. By A. G. Payne.
Poor Relief in Foreign Countries.
Cremation and Urn Burial, Our. By W. Robinson. Illustrated.
Colonies and India, Our. By Prof. Ransome, M.A. Oxon.
Etiquette of Good Society. *New Edition.* Edited and Revised by Lady Colin Campbell. (*Also in cloth,* 1s. 6d.)
Co-operators, Working Men: What they have Done, and What they are Doing.
Photography for Amateurs. By T. C. Hepworth. Illustrated. (*Also in cloth,* 1s. 6d.)
"My Diary." With Coloured Plates and 366 Woodcuts.

CASSELL'S SUNSHINE SERIES. Monthly Volumes.
The Temptation of Dulce Carruthers. By C. E. C. Weigall.
Lady Lorrimer's Scheme and The Story of a Glamour. By Edith E. Cuthell.
WomanliHe. By Florence M. King.
On Stronger Wings. By Edith Lister.
"You'll Love Me Yet." By Frances Haswell; and "That Little Woman." By Ida Lemon.
The Select Works of George Combe. Issued by Authority of the Combe Trustees. *Popular Edition.* Each. (Net.)
The Constitution of Man. | Science and Religion.
Moral Philosophy. | Discussions on Education.
      American Notes.

ILLUSTRATED OFFICIAL RAILWAY GUIDES.

In Paper. (*Also in cloth,* 2s.)
South Eastern.—London, Brighton and South Coast.—London and South Western.—Great Northern.—Midland.—London and North Western (*Revised Edition*).—Great Western (*New and Revised Edition*).—Great Eastern.

RELIGIOUS.

"HEART CHORDS." Bound in cloth, red edges. Each.
My Work for God. | My Hereafter.
My Object in Life. | My Walk with God.
My Aspirations. | My Aids to the Divine Life.
My Emotional Life. | My Sources of Strength.
My Body. | My Father.
My Growth in Divine Life. | My Bible.
      My Soul.

HELPS TO BELIEF. Edited by the Rev. Canon Shore, M.A.
Creation. By the late Lord Bishop of Carlisle.
Prayer. By the Rev. Canon Shore, M.A.
The Divinity of Our Lord. By the Lord Bishop of Derry.
Miracles. By the Rev. Brownlow Maitland, M.A.
The Atonement. By William Connor Magee, D.D., late Archbishop of York.
The Morality of the Old Testament. By the Rev. N. Smyth, D.D.
Hid Treasure. By Richard Harris Hill.
History of Holy Trinity, Minories. By the Rev. Dr. S. Kinns.
Shortened Church Services and Hymns. Compiled by the Rev. T. Teignmouth Shore, M.A., Canon of Worcester.
My Comfort in Sorrow. By Hugh Macmillan, D.D.

1/3

CASSELL'S "JAPANESE" LIBRARY.

Consisting of 12 Popular Works bound in Japanese style. Each. (Net.)
Handy Andy.—Oliver Twist.—Ivanhoe.—Ingoldsby Legends.—The Last of the Mohicans.—The Last Days of Pompeii.—The Yellowplush Papers.—The Last Days of Palmyra.—Jack Hinton, the Guardsman.—Selections from Hood's Works.—American Humour.—Tower of London.

1/4

British Museum, The Bible Student in the. By the Rev. J. G. Kitchin, M.A. *New and Revised Edition.*
School Registers, Cassell's. 1. Attendance Register, 1s. 4d. 2. Admission Register, 10s. 3. Summary Register, 10s.

1/6

Won at the Last Hole. A Golfing Romance. By M. A. Stobart. Illustrated.
Broadacre Farm; or, Lessons in Our Laws. By H. F. Lester. Illustrated.
Facts from the Furrows, or More Talk at Broadacre Farm. Uniform with "Broadacre Farm."
Object Lessons from Nature, for the Use of Schools. By Prof. L. C. Miall. Illustrated. New and enlarged Edition. Two Vols. Each. Also in One Vol., 3s.
University Extension: Past, Present, and Future. By Prof. Mackinder, and M. E. Sadler, M.A. With Maps and Plans.
Vegetarian Cookery. By A. G. Payne.
Cassell's New Poetry Readers. Illustrated. 12 Books in One Vol., cloth. (*See also* 1d.)
Guide to Employment for Boys on leaving School. By W. S. Beard, F.R.G.S.
Engineering Workshop Practice, Forty Lessons in.
Elementary Chemistry for Science Schools and Classes.
Twilight of Life, The. Words of Counsel and Comfort for the Aged. By John Ellerton, M.A.
Laws of Every-Day Life. By H. O. Arnold-Forster, M.P. Cloth.
Citizen Reader. By H. O. Arnold-Forster, M.P. Cloth. (*Presentation Edition,* 3s. 6d.) (*Also a Scottish Edition, cloth,* 1s. 6d.)
Round the Empire. By G. R. Parkin. With a Preface by the Earl of Rosebery, K.G. Fully Illustrated.
The Making of the Home. By Mrs. S. A. Barnett.
Temperance Reader, The. By Rev. J. Dennis Hird.
Little Folks' History of England. By Isa Craig-Knox. With 30 Illustrations. Cloth.
French, Key to Cassell's Lessons in. Cloth.
Khiva, Burnaby's Ride to. Cloth.
Experimental Geometry, First Elements of. By Paul Bert. Illustrated.
Principles of Perspective as Applied to Model Drawing and Sketching from Nature, The. By George Trobridge. (*Cloth,* 2s. 6d.)
Energy and Motion: A Text Book of Elementary Mechanics. By W. Paice, M.A.
Nursing for the Home and for the Hospital, A Handbook of. By C. J. Wood. (*Also in cloth,* 2s.)

GIFT BOOKS FOR YOUNG PEOPLE.

By Popular Authors. With Illustrations in each. Cloth gilt.
The Boy Hunters of Kentucky. By Edward S. Ellis. | Ruth's Life Work; or, "No Pains, no Gains."
Red Feather: a Tale of the American Frontier. By Edward S. Ellis. [Symington. | Rags and Rainbows: a Story of Thanksgiving.
Seeking a City. By Maggie | Uncle William's Charge; or, The Broken Trust.
Rhoda's Reward; or "If Wishes were Horses." | Pretty Pink's Purpose; or, The Little Street Merchants.
Frank's Life-Battle; or, The Three Friends. |
Jack Marston's Anchor. | Trixy; or, "Those who Live in Glass Houses shouldn't Throw Stones."
Fritters; or, "It's a Long Lane that has no Turning." | The Two Hardcastles; or, "A Friend in Need is a Friend Indeed."
Major Monk's Motto; or, "Look before you Leap." |
Ursula's Stumbling Block; or, "Pride comes before a Fall." | Tim Thomson's Trial; or, "All is not Gold that Glitters."

EIGHTEENPENNY STORY BOOKS.

All Illustrated throughout, and bound in cloth gilt.
Wee Willie Winkie. | Girl with the Golden Locks.
Ups and Downs of a Donkey's Life. | The Chip Boy; and other Stories.
Three Wee Ulster Lassies. | Roses from Thorns.
Up the Ladder. | Raggles, Baggles, and the Emperor.
Faith's Father. |
By Land and Sea. | Stories of the Olden Time.
The Young Berringtons. | Dick's Hero; and other Stories.
Tom Morris's Error. |
Worth More than Gold. | The Old Fairy Tales. With Original Illustrations. Cloth.
Jeff and Leff. [Fire. | (*Also in boards,* 1s.)
Through Flood — Through |

THE LIBRARY OF WONDERS.

Illustrated Gift Books for Boys. Crown 8vo, cloth.
Wonderful Adventures. — Wonders of Bodily Strength and Skill.—Wonderful Escapes.—Wonders of Animal Instinct.—Wonderful Balloon Ascents.

1/9

Physiology for Schools. By Alfred T. Schofield, M.D., M.R.C.S., &c. Illustrated. Cloth. (*Also in Three Parts, paper covers,* 3d. *each; or cloth limp,* 6d. *each.*)

2/-

EDUCATIONAL.

Historical Cartoons, Cassell's Coloured. (Size 45 in. × 35 in.) Six. Each. (*See also* 1d. *and* 5s.)
Higher Class Readers, Cassell's. Illustrated. Cloth. Each. (*Also cloth gilt,* 2s. 6d.)
Practical Solid Geometry, A Manual of. By William Gordon Ross, Major R.E.
Applied Mechanics. By Sir R. Stawell Ball, LL.D.
Linear Drawing. By E. A. Davidson.
Orthographic and Isometrical Projection.
Building Construction, The Elements of.
Systematic Drawing and Shading. By Charles Ryan.
Jones's Book-keeping. By Theodore Jones. For Schools, 2s.; for the Million, 2s. (*Also in cloth,* 3s.) Ruled Books, 2s.
History of England for Elementary Schools. Illustrated. (*See also* 10d. *and* 1s.)
Reading Sheets, Modern. 3 Series. Each. (*Also on linen, with rollers,* 5s. *each.*)

2/-
cont'd.

CASSELL'S STANDARD LIBRARY. Cloth. Each.

Shirley.
Coningsby.
Mary Barton.
The Antiquary.
Nicholas Nickleby. (2 Vols.)
Jane Eyre.
Wuthering Heights.
The Prairie.
Dombey and Son. (2 Vols.)
Night and Morning.
Kenilworth.
Ingoldsby Legends.
Tower of London.
The Pioneers.
Charles O'Malley.
Barnaby Rudge.
Cakes and Ale.
The King's Own.
People I have Met.
The Pathfinder.
Evelina.
Scott's Poems.
Last of the Barons.
Adventures of Mr. Ledbury.
Ivanhoe.
Oliver Twist.
Selections from Thomas Hood's Works.
Longfellow's Prose Works.
Sense and Sensibility.
Lord Lytton's Plays.
Bret Harte—Tales, Poems, &c.
Martin Chuzzlewit. (2 Vols.)
The Prince of the House of David.
Sheridan's Plays.
Uncle Tom's Cabin.
Eugene Aram.
Jack Hinton, the Guardsman.
Rome and the Early Christians.
Thackeray's Yellowplush Papers.
Deerslayer.
Washington Irving's Sketch Book.
Last Days of Palmyra.
Tales of the Borders.
Pride and Prejudice.
Last of the Mohicans.
The Old Curiosity Shop.
Rienzi.
The Talisman.
The Heart of Midlothian.
The Last Days of Pompeii.
Sketches by Boz.
American Humour.
Macaulay's Lays and Selected Essays.
Harry Lorrequer.
The Pickwick Papers (2 Vols.)
Scarlet Letter.
Handy Andy.
The Hour and the Man.
Old Mortality.
Edgar Allan Poe. (Prose and Poetry, Selections from.)
Margaret Lyndsay.

CASSELL'S RAILWAY LIBRARY. Crown 8vo, paper.

Metzerott, Shoemaker. By Katharine Woods.
David Todd. By David Maclure.
The Admirable Lady Biddy Fane. By Frank Barrett.
Commodore Junk. By G. Manville Fenn.
St. Cuthbert's Tower. By Florence Warden.
The Man with a Thumb. By W. C. Hudson (Barclay North).
By Right Not Law. By R. Sherard.
Within Sound of the Weir. By Thomas St. E. Hake.
The Coombsberrow Mystery. By James Colwall.
Under a Strange Mask. By Frank Barrett.
A Queer Race. By W. Westall.
Captain Trafalgar. By Westall and Laurie. [Westall.
The Phantom City. By W.
Jack Gordon, Knight Errant. By W. C. Hudson.
A Tragic Mystery. By Julian Hawthorne.
The Diamond Button: Whose was It? By W. C. Hudson.
Another's Crime. By Julian Hawthorne.
The Yoke of the Thorah. By Henry Harland.
The Tragedy of Brinkwater. By Martha L. Moodey.
Who is John Noman? By Charles Henry Beckett.
An American Penman. By Julian Hawthorne.
Section 558; or, The Fatal Letter. By Julian Hawthorne.
The Brown Stone Boy. By W. H. Bishop.
The Great Bank Robbery. By Julian Hawthorne.

G. MANVILLE FENN'S NOVELS.

Cheap Edition. In paper boards.

The Parson o' Dumford. }
The Vicar's People. } In paper boards only.

My Patients. Being the Notes of a Navy Surgeon; also cloth boards, 2s. 6d.

Poverty Corner. Also Cloth boards, 2s. 6d.

MISCELLANEOUS.

Hiram Golf's Religion; or, The Shoemaker by the Grace of God.
The Breech-loader, and How to Use It. By W. W. Greener. Illustrated.
Cassell's Popular Cookery. With Coloured Plates.
A Guide to Health. For the Use of Soldiers. By Surgeon-Major R. C. Eaton, Medical Staff.
The Voter's Handbook. By W. V. R. Fane (of the Inner Temple) and A. H. Graham (of the Middle Temple). Cloth limp.
How Dante Climbed the Mountain. By R. E. Selfe. Illustrated.
Morning and Evening Prayers for Workhouses and other Institutions. Selected by Louisa Twining.
Cassell's Book of In-door Amusements, Card Games, and Fireside Fun. Illustrated.
John Orlebar, Clk. By the Author of "Culmshire Folk."
"Little Folks" Proverb Painting Book.

THE "GOLDEN MOTTOES" SERIES.

Each Book containing 208 pages, with Four full-page Original Illustrations. Crown 8vo, cloth gilt.

"Nil Desperandum." By the Rev. F. Langbridge, M.A.
"Bear and Forbear." By Sarah Pitt.
"He Conquers who Endures." By the Author of "May Cunningham's Trial," &c.
"Honour is my Guide." By Jeanie Hering (Mrs. Adams-Acton).
"Aim at the Sure End." By Emily Searchfield.
"Foremost if I Can." By Helen Atteridge.

TWO-SHILLING STORY BOOKS.

All Illustrated throughout, and containing Stories for Young People. Crown 8vo, handsomely bound in cloth gilt.

The Top of the Ladder: How to Reach it.
Stories of the Tower.
Mr. Burke's Nieces.
May Cunningham's Trial.
Peggy, and other Tales.
"Little Folks" Sunday Book.
The Children of the Court.
Four Cats of the Tippertons.
Marion's Two Homes.
Little Flotsam.
Madge and her Friends.
Through Peril to Fortune.
Aunt Tabitha's Waifs.
In Mischief Again.
Two Fourpenny Bits.
Poor Nelly.
Tom Heriot.
Maid Marjory.

2/6

CASSELL'S MINIATURE LIBRARY OF THE POETS.

In Two Volumes, cloth, gilt edges, in Paper Box, per set. (*See also* 1s.)

Milton - 2 Vols.
Wordsworth - 2 Vols.
Longfellow - 2 Vols.
Scott - 2 Vols.
Hood - 2 Vols.
Burns - 2 Vols
Byron - 2 Vols.
Sheridan and Goldsmith } 2 Vols.

Shakespeare's Plays. The Seven Plays produced at the Lyceum, in paper box.

2/6
cont'd.

"WANTED—A KING" SERIES.

Cheap Edition. Illustrated.

Fairy Tales in Other Lands. By Julia Goddard.
Robin's Ride. By Ellinor Davenport Adams.
Great-Grandmamma. By Georgina M. Synge.
Wanted—a King; or, How Merle set the Nursery Rhymes to Rights. By Maggie Browne.

BIBLE BIOGRAPHIES. Illustrated.

The Story of Joseph. By the Rev. George Bainton.
The Story of Moses and Joshua. By the Rev. J. Telford.
The Story of Judges. By the Rev. J. Wycliffe Gedge.
The Story of Samuel and Saul. By the Rev. D. C. Tovey.
The Story of David. By the Rev. J. Wild.
The Story of Jesus. In Verse. By J. R. Macduff, D.D.

THE "CROSS AND CROWN" SERIES.

With Four Illustrations in each Book printed on a Tint.

In Letters of Flame.
Through Trial to Triumph.
Heroes of the Indian Empire.
Strong to Suffer.
By Fire and Sword: A Story of the Huguenots.
Adam Hepburn's Vow.
No. XIII.; or, the Story of the Lost Vestal.

BOOKS BY EDWARD S. ELLIS. Illustrated.

The Hunters of the Ozark.
The Camp in the Mountains.
The Last War Trail.
Ned in the Woods.
Ned on the River.
Ned in the Block House: A Story of Pioneer Life in Kentucky.
The Lost Trail.
Camp-Fire and Wigwam.
Foot-prints in the Forest.
Down the Mississippi.
Lost in the Wilds.
Up the Tapajos: or, Adventures in Brazil.

THE WORLD IN PICTURES.

Handsomely Illustrated, and elegantly bound.

A Ramble Round France.
All the Russias.
Chats about Germany.
The Eastern Wonderland.
Peeps into China.
The Land of the Pyramids (Egypt).
Glimpses of South America.
Round Africa.
The Land of Temples.
The Isles of the Pacific.

HALF-CROWN GIFT BOOKS.

Illustrated. Crown 8vo, cloth gilt.

Pen's Perplexities.
Margaret's Enemy.
Notable Shipwrecks.
Wonders of Common Things.
Soldier and Patriot.
The Young Man in the Battle of Life.
Truth will Out.

POPULAR VOLUMES FOR YOUNG PEOPLE.

Maggie Steele's Diary. By E. A. Dillwyn.
The Peep of Day. An Old Friend in a New Dress. Illustrated.
Schoolroom and Home Theatricals. By Arthur Waugh. With Illustrations by H. J. A. Miles.
Wild Adventures in Wild Places. By Dr. Gordon Stables, R.N. Illustrated.
Pictures of School Life and Boyhood. Selected from the best Authors. Edited by Percy Fitzgerald, M.A.
Perils Afloat and Brigands Ashore. By Alfred Elwes.
Freedom's Sword: A Story of the Days of Wallace and Bruce. By Annie S. Swan.
Modern Explorers. By T. Frost. Illustrated.
Decisive Events in History. By Thomas Archer. Illustrated.
The True Robinson Crusoes. Cloth gilt.
Early Explorers. By Thomas Frost. Illustrated.
Home Chat with our Young Folks. Illustrated throughout.
Jungle, Peak, and Plain. Illustrated throughout.
Peeps Abroad for Folks at Home. Illustrated.
The World's Lumber Room. By Selina Gaye.
Heroes of Every-day Life. By Laura Lane. Illustrated.
Short Studies from Nature. Illustrated.
Rambles Round London. By C. L. Matéaux.
Around and About Old England. By C. L. Matéaux.
For Queen and King. By Henry Frith. Illustrated.
Esther West. By Isa Craig-Knox. Illustrated.
Three Homes. By F. L. T. Hope. Illustrated.
Working to Win. By Maggie Symington. Illustrated.
Paws and Claws. By one of the Authors of "Poems Written for a Child."
In Quest of Gold: or, Under the Whanga Falls.
On Board the "Esmeralda"; or, Martin Leigh's Log.
The Romance of Invention: Vignettes from the Annals of Industry and Science.

EDUCATIONAL.

Agriculture Text-Books, Cassell's. (The "Downton" Series.) Edited by John Wrightson, M.R.A.C., F.C.S., Professor of Agriculture. Fully Illustrated. Each.
Farm Crops. By Professor Wrightson.
Soils and Manures. By J. M. H. Munro, D.Sc. (Lond.), F.I.C., F.C.S.
Live Stock. By Professor Wrightson.
Cassell's Popular Atlas. Containing 24 Coloured Maps.
Cassell's Classical Texts for Schools, from 2s. 6d. to 4s. (*A list post free on application.*)
Sculpture, A Primer of. By E. R. Mullins.
Numerical Examples in Practical Mechanics and Machine Design. By R. G. Blaine, M.E. *New Edition, Revised and Enlarged.* With 79 Illustrations.
Latin Primer (The New). By Prof. J. P. Postgate.
Latin Prose for Lower Forms. By M. A. Bayfield, M.A.
Chemistry, The Public School. By J. H. Anderson, M.A.
Oil Painting, A Manual of. By the Hon. John Collier. Cloth.
French Reader, Cassell's Public School. By Guillaume S. Conrad.
French Grammar, Marlborough. Arranged and Compiled by Rev. J. F. Bright, M.A. (*See* "Exercises," 3s. 6d.)
Algebra, Manual of. By Galbraith and Haughton. Part I. Cloth. (*Complete,* 7s. 6d.)
Optics. By Galbraith and Haughton.
Euclid. Books I., II., III. By Galbraith and Haughton.
—————— Books IV., V., VI. By Galbraith and Haughton.
Plane Trigonometry. By Galbraith and Haughton. Cloth.
French, Cassell's Lessons in. Parts I. and II. Cloth. Each. (*Complete,* 4s. 6d.)
"Model Joint" Wall Sheets, for Instruction in Manual Training. By S. Barter. Eight Sheets. Each.
Natural History Wall Sheets (Cassell's). Ten Subjects. Separate Sheets, 2s. 6d. each. *Unmounted,* 2s. each. (*See also* 20s. and 25s.)

2/6 cont'd.

MISCELLANEOUS.

Cottage Gardening, Poultry, Bees, Allotments, Food, House, Window and Town Gardens. Edited by W. ROBINSON, F.L.S., Author of "The English Flower Garden." Fully Illustrated. Half-yearly Volumes I. and II. Each.

Liquor Legislation in the United States and Canada. By E. L. Fanshawe, of the Inner Temple, Barrister.

Field Naturalist's Handbook, The. By the Revs. J. G. Wood and Theodore Wood. *Cheap Edition.*

The Manual of the Guild and School of Handicraft. Edited by C. R. Ashbee, M.A.

The Art of Making and Using Sketches. From the French of G. FRAIPONT. By Clara Bell. With Fifty Illustrations.

Geometrical Drawing for Army Candidates. By H. T. Lilley, M.A. *New and Enlarged Edition.*

Elizabeth Gilbert and her Work for the Blind. By Frances Martin.

Father Mathew: His Life and Times. By F. J. Mathew.

Free Public Libraries. By Thomas Greenwood, F.R.G.S. *New and Enlarged Edition.* Illustrated.

Colonist's Medical Handbook, The. By E. A. Barton, M.R.C.S.

Nursing of Sick Children, A Handbook for the. By Catherine J. Wood.

Browning, An Introduction to the Study of. By Arthur Symons.

The England of Shakespeare. By E. Goadby. Illustrated.

At the South Pole. By W. H. G. Kingston. Illustrated.

Ships, Sailors, and the Sea. By R. J. Cornewall-Jones. Illustrated. *Cheap Edition.*

Unicode. The Universal Telegraphic Phrase Book. Desk and Pocket Editions. Each.

Bo-Peep. A Treasury for the Little Ones. Yearly Volume. Boards. (*See* 3s. 6d.)

Sent Back by the Angels, and other Ballads. By the Rev. F. Langbridge, M.A. Cloth.

New Testament, An Introduction to the.

Miniature Cyclopædia, Cassell's. Containing 30,000 Subjects. Cloth. (*Also in half roxburgh*, 4s.)

3/-

TECHNICAL MANUALS (Illustrated).

The Elements of Practical Perspective.	Drawing for Cabinetmakers.
Model Drawing.	Drawing for Bricklayers.
Drawing for Stonemasons.	Drawing for Metal-Plate Workers.

Gothic Stonework.

Cassell's New Coloured Natural History Wall Sheets. Consisting of 18 Subjects. Size—39 by 31 in. Mounted on rollers and varnished. Each.

How to Shade from Models, Common Objects, and Casts of Ornament. A Practical Manual. By W. E. Sparkes.

Practical Plane and Solid Geometry, including Graphic Arithmetic. Vol. I., Elementary Stage.

Elementary Flower Painting. With Eight Coloured Plates and Wood Engravings.

Sepia Painting, A Course of. Two Vols. Each. (*In one Vol.,* 5s.)

Marlborough Arithmetic Examples.

Tides and Tidal Currents. By Galbraith and Haughton.

SCHOOL COMMENTARIES. Edited by Bishop Ellicott.

Genesis. (3s. 6d.)	Romans. (2s. 6d.)
Exodus. (3s.)	Corinthians I. and II. (3s.)
Leviticus. (3s.)	Galatians, Ephesians, and
Numbers. (2s. 6d.)	Philippians. (3s.)
Deuteronomy. (2s. 6d.)	Colossians, Thessalonians, and Timothy. (3s.)
St. Matthew. (3s. 6d.)	Titus, Philemon, Hebrews, and James. (3s.)
St. Mark. (3s.)	Peter, Jude, and John. (3s.)
St. Luke. (3s. 6d.)	The Revelation. (3s.)
St. John. (3s. 6d.)	An Introduction to the New Testament. (2s. 6d.)
The Acts of the Apostles. (3s. 6d.)	

THE WORLD'S WORKERS.

New and Original Volumes by Popular Authors. With Portraits. In Seven Vols., each containing 3 works. Cloth, gilt edges. Each Vol.

*** Each work can also be had separately. (*See* 1s.)

Biblewomen and Nurses. Yearly Volume.

3/6

EDUCATIONAL.

Cassell's English Dictionary. Giving Definitions of more than 100,000 Words and Phrases. *Cheap Edition.*

Drawing for Carpenters and Joiners. By E. A. Davidson. With 253 Engravings.

Natural Philosophy. By Prof. Haughton.

Practical Mechanics. By Prof. Perry, M.E.

Cutting Tools Worked by Hand and Machine. By Prof. Smith.

Handrailing and Staircasing. By Frank O. Cresswell.

Hydrostatics. By Galbraith and Haughton. Cloth.

Steam Engine. By Galbraith and Haughton. Cloth.

Mathematical Tables. By Galbraith and Haughton.

Mechanics. By Galbraith and Haughton. Cloth.

Linear Drawing and Projection. Two Vols. in One.

German Dictionary, Cassell's NEW. In Two Parts. German-English and English-German. Cloth. (*Also in half roan*, 4s. 6d.)

This World of Ours. By H. O. Arnold-Forster, M.P. Being Introductory Lessons to the Study of Geography.

Commercial Botany of the Nineteenth Century. By J. R. Jackson, A.L.S.

Colour. By Prof. A. H. Church. *New and Enlarged Edition.*

English Literature, The Story of. By Anna Buckland.

Guide to Employment in the Civil Service. Cloth.

Italian Grammar, The Elements of, with Exercises.

German Grammar, The Marlborough. Compiled and Arranged by the Rev. J. F. Bright, M.A. Cloth.

French Exercises, Marlborough. By the Rev. G. W. De Lisle, M.A., French Master in Marlborough College.

French-English and English-French Dictionary. *Revised Edition*, with 3,000 new words. Cloth. (*Also in superior binding, with leather backs.* 4s. 6d.)

Cassell's New Latin Dictionary. (Latin-English and English-Latin.) Revised by J. R. V. Marchant, M.A., and J. F. Charles, B.A.

Phrase and Fable, Dictionary of. By Rev. E. C. Brewer, LL.D. *Twentieth Edition, Enlarged.* (*See also* 4s. 6d.)

Alphabet, Cassell's Pictorial, and Object Lesson Sheet for Infant Schools.

3/6 cont'd.

THE FIGUIER SERIES.

Cheap Editions. Illustrated throughout.

The Insect World.	The Ocean World.
Reptiles and Birds.	The World before the Deluge.
The Human Race.	Mammalia.

The Vegetable World.

Some Legendary Landmarks of Africa. By Mrs. Frank Evans.

New England Boyhood, A. By Edward E. Hale.

Scarabæus; the Story of an African Beetle. By the Marquise Clara Lanza and James Clarence Harvey. *Cheap Edition.*

Fairway Island. By Horace Hutchinson. Illustrated. *Cheap Edition.*

Old and New Testaments, Plain Introductions to the Books of the. Reprinted from Bishop Ellicott's Bible Commentary. In Two Volumes. Each.

Joy and Health. Poems by Martellius. Illustrated. (Also an *Edition de Luxe*, 7s. 6d.)

Story Poems for Young and Old. Edited by E. Davenport. *Cheap Edition.*

Shaftesbury, K.G., The Seventh Earl of, The Life and Work of. By Edwin Hodder. Illustrated. *Cheap Edition.*

The Lady's Dressing-Room. Translated from the French by Lady Colin Campbell.

Beetles, Butterflies, Moths, and other Insects. By A. W. Kappel, F.L.S., F.E.S., and W. Egmont Kirby. With Twelve Coloured Plates.

Nature's Wonder Workers. By Kate R. Lovell. Illustrated.

The Perfect Gentleman. By the Rev. A. Smythe-Palmer, D.D.

The Successful Life. A Book for Young Men commencing Business, containing Counsel, Instruction, Comfort. By an Elder Brother.

The Carnation Manual. Edited and Issued by the National Carnation and Picotee Society (Southern Section).

Artistic Anatomy. By Prof. M. Duval. *Cheap Edition.*

The English School of Painting. *Cheap Edition.*

Buckinghamshire Sketches. By E. S. Roscoe. With Illustrations by H. R. Bloomer. Cloth.

Verses Grave and Gay. By Ellen Thorneycroft Fowler.

Italy from the Fall of Napoleon I. in 1815 to 1890. By J. W. Probyn. *New and Cheaper Edition.*

Heroes of Britain in Peace and War. *Cheap Edition.* Two Vols. With 300 Illustrations. Each. (*See also* 7s. 6d.)

Disraeli, Benjamin, The Rt. Hon. Earl of Beaconsfield, K.G., Personal Reminiscences of. By Henry Lake. With Two Portraits, &c.

Life of Nelson. By Robert Southey. Illustrated.

The Law of Musical and Dramatic Copyright. *New Edition.*

Aubrey de Vere's Poems. A Selection. Edited by John Dennis.

Gas, The Art of Cooking by. By Marie Jenny Sugg. Illustrated.

London. Three large Maps, viz.: London as it is, and as it was in 1720, and in the reign of Elizabeth. In case.

Marriage Ring, The. A Gift Book for the Newly Married and for those Contemplating Marriage. By William Landels, D.D.

Lectures on Christianity and Socialism. By the Right Rev. Alfred Barry, D.D.

Shakspere, The Leopold. With about 400 Illustrations. Cloth. (*Also at* 5s. *and* 7s. 6d.)

Culmshire Folk. By the Author of "John Orlebar," &c.

Steam Engine, The Theory and Action of the. FOR PRACTICAL MEN. By W. H. Northcott, C.E.

A Year's Cookery. By Phyllis Browne. *New and Enlarged Edition.*

Sports and Pastimes, Cassell's Complete Book of. *Cheap Edition.* With over 900 Illustrations. Cloth.

Poultry-Keeper, The Practical. By Lewis Wright. With Numerous Woodcuts.

Pigeon Keeper, The Practical. By Lewis Wright.

Rabbit Keeper, The Practical. By Cuniculus.

Bunyan's Pilgrim's Progress, Cassell's. Illustrated. Cloth. (*Also cloth gilt, gilt edges,* 5s.)

THE "TREASURE ISLAND" SERIES.

CHEAP ILLUSTRATED EDITIONS.

Treasure Island. By R. L. Stevenson.

The Master of Ballantrae. By R. L. Stevenson.

"Kidnapped." By R. L. Stevenson.

The Black Arrow. By R. L. Stevenson.

King Solomon's Mines. By H. Rider Haggard.

YOUNG PEOPLE'S STORY BOOKS.

Cheap Edition. With Original Illustrations. Cloth gilt.

Under Bayard's Banner. By Henry Frith.

The Champion of Odin; or, Viking Life in the Days of Old. By J. Frederick Hodgetts.

Bound by a Spell; or, The Hunted Witch of the Forest. By the Hon. Mrs. Greene.

BOOKS FOR YOUNG PEOPLE.

A Sunday Story-Book. By Maggie Browne, Sam Browne, and Aunt Ethel. Illustrated.

A Bundle of Tales. By Maggie Browne, Sam Browne, and Aunt Ethel.

The Sunday Scrap-Book. Containing several hundred Scripture Stories in Pictures. Boards. (*Also in cloth,* 5s.)

Little Mother Bunch. By Mrs. Molesworth. Illustrated.

Æsop's Fables. *Cheap Edition.* Cloth. (*Also in cloth, bevelled boards, gilt edges,* 5s.)

Rhymes for the Young Folk. By William Allingham. Boards.

The Chit-Chat Album. Illustrated throughout.

Picture Album of All Sorts. With Full-page Illustrations.

My Own Album of Animals.

Album for Home, School, and Play. Containing numerous Stories by popular Authors.

Cassell's Pictorial Scrap Book. In Six Sectional Volumes, paper boards, cloth back. Each Vol.

Bo-Peep. A Treasury for the Little Ones. Illustrated throughout. Cloth gilt. Yearly Volume. (*See also* 2s. 6d.)

3/6 cont'd.

Robinson Crusoe, Cassell's. Profusely Illustrated. Cloth. (*Also in cloth, bevelled boards, gilt edges,* 5s.)
Swiss Family Robinson, Cassell's. Illustrated. Cloth. (*Also in cloth, bevelled boards, gilt edges,* 5s.)
Vicar of Wakefield, The, and other Works by Goldsmith. Illustrated. (*Also in cloth, gilt edges,* 5s.)
Gulliver's Travels. *Cheap Edition.* With Eighty-eight Engravings by Morten. Crown 4to, cloth. (*Also in cloth, gilt edges,* 5s.)
Little Folks (ENLARGED SERIES). Half-Yearly Vols. With Pictures on nearly every page, together with two Full-page Plates printed in Colours, and Four Tinted Plates. Coloured boards. (*See also* 5s.)

POPULAR BOOKS FOR YOUNG PEOPLE.
Crown 8vo, with Eight Full-page Illustrations. Cloth gilt.

† **Bashful Fifteen.** By L. T. Meade. Illustrated.
† **A Sweet Girl Graduate.** By L. T. Meade. Illustrated.
† **The White House at Inch Gow.** By Sarah Pitt. Illustrated.
The King's Command: A Story for Girls. By Maggie Symington. Illustrated. *Cheap Edition.*
Lost in Samoa. A Tale of Adventure in the Navigator Islands. By E. S. Ellis. With Eight Original Illustrations.
Tad; or, "Getting Even" with Him. By E. S. Ellis. With Eight Original Illustrations.
† **Polly: A New-fashioned Girl.** By L. T. Meade. Illustrated.
† **A World of Girls: A Story of a School.** By L. T. Meade.
† **The Palace Beautiful.** A Story for Girls. By L. T. Meade.
† **The Cost of a Mistake.** By Sarah Pitt. Illustrated.
Lost among White Africans: A Boy's Adventures on the Upper Congo. By David Ker.
For Fortune and Glory. A Story of the Soudan War. By Lewis Hough.
"Follow my Leader"; or, The Boys of Templeton. By Talbot Baines Reed.
Books marked thus † can also be had in superior bindings, extra cloth gilt, gilt edges, 5s. *each.*

4/-

National Railways. An Argument for State Purchase. By James Hole. Net.
Work. The Illustrated Journal for Mechanics. *New and Enlarged Series.* Vol. V.
Zero, the Slaver. A Romance of Equatorial Africa. By Lawrence Fletcher.
Into the Unknown: A Romance of South Africa. By Lawrence Fletcher.
A Daughter of the South, and Shorter Stories. By Mrs. Burton Harrison.
"Eli Perkins." Thirty Years of Wit. By Melville D. Landon ("Eli Perkins").
Cassell's Classical Texts for Schools, from 2s. 6d. to 4s. (*A list post free on application.*)

4/6

Mechanics for Young Beginners, A First Book of. With numerous Easy Examples and Answers. By the Rev. J. G. Easton, M.A.
Watch and Clock Making. By D. Glasgow, Vice-President of the British Horological Institute.
Design in Textile Fabrics. By T. R. Ashenhurst. With Coloured and numerous other Illustrations.
Spinning Woollen and Worsted. By W. S. B. McLaren, M.P.
Phrase and Fable, Dictionary of. *New and Enlarged Edition.* By the Rev. Dr. Brewer. Superior binding. (*See also* 3s. 6d.)
French, Cassell's Lessons in. *New and Revised Edition.* Complete in One Vol. (*See also* 2s. 6d.)
Drawing for Machinists and Engineers. By Ellis A. Davidson. With over 200 Illustrations.

5/-

ILLUSTRATED BOOKS FOR YOUNG PEOPLE.
Pleasant Work for Busy Fingers; or, Kindergarten at Home. By Maggie Browne. Illustrated.
London Street Arabs. By Mrs. H. M. Stanley (Dorothy Tennant).
Magic at Home. By Prof. Hoffman. Fully Illustrated.
Flora's Feast. A Masque of Flowers. By Walter Crane. With 40 pages in Colours.
"Come, ye Children." By Rev. Benjamin Waugh. Illustrated.
Little Folks. Half-Yearly Vols. *New and Enlarged Series.* With Pictures on nearly every page, together with Two Full-page Plates printed in Colours, and Four Tinted Plates. Cloth gilt, gilt edges. (*See also* 3s. 6d.)

EDUCATIONAL.
Storehouse of General Information, Cassell's. Fully Illustrated. In Vols. Each.
Popular Educator, Cassell's NEW. With Revised Text, New Maps, New Coloured Plates, New Type &c. Complete in Eight Vols. Each. (*See also* 50s.)
Technical Educator, Cassell's New. An entirely New Cyclopædia of Technical Education, with Coloured Plates and Engravings. In Volumes.
Gaudeamus. Songs for Colleges and Schools. Edited by John Farmer. (The words only, in paper covers, 6d.; cloth, 9d.) Can also be obtained in sheets containing two Songs (words and music) in quantities of one dozen and upwards, at 1d. per sheet.
Dulce Domum. Rhymes and Songs for Children. Edited by John Farmer. Old Notation and Words. *N.B.—the Words of the Songs in "Dulce Domum" (with the Airs both in Tonic Sol Fa and Old Notation) can be had in two parts,* 6d. *each.*
Historical Cartoons, Cassell's Coloured. Six. Mounted on canvas and varnished, with rollers. Each. (*See also* 1d. *and* 2s.)
Howard's Anglo-American Art of Reckoning. By C. Frusher Howard. *New Edition, Enlarged.* (*See also* 1s. *and* 2s.)
Dyeing of Textile Fabrics, The. By Prof. Hummel.
Steel and Iron. By Prof. W. H. Greenwood, F.C.S., &c.
Marine Painting. By Walter W. May, R.I. With Sixteen Coloured Plates.
Animal Painting in Water-Colours. With Eighteen Coloured Plates by Frederick Tayler.
Tree Painting in Water-Colours. By W. H. J. Boot. With Eighteen Coloured Plates.
Water-Colour Painting Book. By R. P. Leitch. With Coloured Plates.

5/- cont'd.

Neutral Tint, A Course of Painting in. With Twenty-four Plates by R. P. Leitch.
China Painting. By Florence Lewis. With Sixteen Original Coloured Plates.
Flowers, and How to Paint them. By Maud Naftel. With Ten Coloured Plates.

RELIGIOUS.
Signa Christi. Evidences of Christianity set forth in the Person and Work of Christ. By the Rev. James Aitchison.
St. George for England: and other Sermons preached to Children. By the Rev. Canon Teignmouth Shore, M.A.
Life of the World to Come, The, and other Subjects. By the Rev. Canon Teignmouth Shore, M.A.
Family Prayer-Book, The. Edited by Rev. Canon Garbett, M.A., and Rev. S. Martin. (*Also in morocco,* 18s.)
Bible, The Pew. Cloth, red edges. (*Also in French morocco,* 6s.; French morocco, gilt edges, 7s.; Persian calf, 7s. 6d.; Persian "Yapp," 8s.; morocco, 8s. 6d.)

The Life of the Rev. J. G. Wood. By his son, the Rev. Theodore Wood. With Portrait. *Cheap Edition.*
Russia. By Sir Donald Mackenzie Wallace, M.A. *Popular Edition.*
Q's Works, Uniform Edition of.

Dead Man's Rock.	The Blue Pavilions.
The Splendid Spur.	"I Saw Three Ships," and
The Astonishing History	other Winter's Tales.
of Troy Town.	Noughts and Crosses.

"SHORT STORY" LIBRARY.
Otto the Knight; and other Stories. By Octave Thanet.
Eleven Possible Cases. By various Authors.
A Singer's Wife. By Fanny N. D. Murfree.
The Poet's Audience, and Delilah. By Clara Savile Clarke.
O'Driscoll's Weird, and other Stories. By A. Werner.
The Book of Pity and of Death. By Pierre Loti. Translated by T. P. O'Connor, M.P.
The Reputation of George Saxon. By Morley Roberts.
Playthings and Parodies. Short Stories, Sketches, &c., by Barry Pain.

Anthea. By Cécile Cassavetti (A Russian). A story of the time of the Greek War of Independence. *Cheap Edition.*
Awkward Squads, The; and other Ulster Stories. By Shan F. Bullock.
Beyond the Blue Mountains. Illustrated. By L. T. Meade.
Capture of the "Estrella," The. A Tale of the Slave Trade. By Commander Claud Harding, R.N.
Iron Pirate, The. A Plain Tale of Strange Happenings on the Sea. By Max Pemberton. Illustrated.
Quickening of Caliban, The. A Modern Story of Evolution. By J. Compton Rickett.
Tenting on the Plains; or, General Custer in Kansas and Texas. By Elizabeth B. Custer. With Numerous Illustrations.
John Drummond Fraser. By Philalethes. A Story of Jesuit Intrigue in the Church of England.
The Shadow of a Song. A Novel. By Cecil Harley.
The Rovings of a Restless Boy. By Katharine B. Foot. Illustrated.
Bob Lovell's Career. A Story of American Railway Life. By Edward S. Ellis.
Mount Desolation. An Australian Romance. By W. Carlton Dawe.
Industrial Freedom: A Study in Politics. By B. R. Wise.
A Blot of Ink. Translated by Q and Paul Francke.
The Doings of Raffles Haw. By A. Conan Doyle, Author of "Sherlock Holmes," &c. *New Edition.*
"Hors de Combat"; or, Three Weeks in a Hospital. Founded on Facts. By Gertrude and Ethel Southam. Illustrated.
Locomotive Engine, The Biography of a. By Henry Frith. Illustrated.
Loans Manual. A Compilation of Tables and Rules for the Use of Local Authorities. By Charles P. Cotton, M.Inst.C.E., M.R.I.A.
Strange Doings in Strange Places. Complete Sensational Stories.
Birds' Nests, Eggs, and Egg-Collecting. By R. Kearton. With 16 Coloured Plates of Eggs.
Modern Shot Guns. By W. W. Greener. Illustrated.
English Writers. By Prof. H. Morley. Vols. I. to X. Each.
Free Trade versus Fair Trade. By the Rt. Hon. Lord Farrer.
Vaccination Vindicated. By John C. McVail, M.D.
Medical and Clinical Manuals, or Practitioners and Students of Medicine. *A List post free on application.* (*Also at* 7s. 6d., 8s. 6d., *and* 9s.)
Household, Cassell's Book of the. In Four Vols. Each. (*See also* 25s.)
Gardening, Cassell's Popular. Illustrated. Complete in Four Vols. Each.
Brahma Fowl, The. By Lewis Wright. With Chromo Plates.

6/-

INTERNATIONAL COPYRIGHT NOVELS.
Extra crown 8vo, cloth. Each.

A Prison Princess. By Major Arthur Griffiths.
The Medicine Lady. By L. T. Meade.
Out of the Jaws of Death. By Frank Barrett.
A Modern Dick Whittington. By James Payn.
The Snare of the Fowler. By Mrs. Alexander.
The Squire. By Mrs. Parr.
The Little Minister. By J. M. Barrie. *Illustrated Edition.*
The Wrecker. By Robert Louis Stevenson and Lloyd Osbourne. Illustrated.
Catriona. A Sequel to "Kidnapped." By Robert Louis Stevenson.
Island Nights' Entertainments. By R. L. Stevenson. Illustrated.
Leona. By Mrs. Molesworth.
The New Ohio. A Story of East and West. By Edward Everett Hale.
Sybil Knox, or Home Again: a Story of To-Day. By Edward E. Hale, Author of "East and West," &c.
The Story of Francis Cludde. By Stanley J. Weyman, Author of "The House of the Wolf" &c. &c.
The Faith Doctor. By Dr. Edward Eggleston.
Dr. Dumány's Wife. By Maurus Jókai, Author of "Timar's Two Worlds." Translated from the Hungarian by F. Steinitz.

Delectable Duchy, The. Some Tales of East Cornwall. By Q.
A Foot-Note to History: Eight Years of Trouble in Samoa. By R. L. Stevenson.
"La Bella," and Others. Being Certain Stories Recollected by Egerton Castle, Author of "Consequences."

6/- cont'd.

Europe, Cassell's Pocket Guide to. Edition for 1893. Leather.

The Nature and Elements of Poetry. By E. C. Stedman.

Star-Land. By Sir Robert Stawell Ball, LL.D. Illustrated.

Queen Summer ; or, The Tourney of the Lily and the Rose. Containing 40 pages of Designs by Walter Crane, printed in Colours.

Fourteen to One ; and other Stories. By Elizabeth Stuart Phelps.

Father Stafford. A Novel. By Anthony Hope.

Teaching in Three Continents. Personal Notes on the Educational Systems of the World. By W. C. Grasby.

Gleanings after Harvest. By the Rev. John R. Vernon, M.A.

St. Paul, The Life and Work of. By the Ven. Archdeacon Farrar, D.D., F.R.S. *Popular Edition.* Cloth. (*See also* 7s. 6d., 10s. 6d., 15s., 21s., 24s., *and* 42s.)

Early Days of Christianity, The. By the Ven. Archdeacon Farrar, D.D., F.R.S. *Popular Edition.* Cloth. (*See also* 7s. 6d., 10s. 6d., 15s., 24s., *and* 42s.)

Life of Christ, The. By the Ven. Archdeacon Farrar, D.D., F.R.S. *Popular Edition.* Cloth. (*See also* 7s. 6d., 10s. 6d., 15s., 24s., *and* 42s.)

Irish Leagues, The Work of the. The Speech of the Right Hon. Sir Henry James, Q.C., M.P., Replying in the Parnell Commission Inquiry.

Hand-and-Eye Training. By G. Ricks, B.Sc. Two Vols., with Sixteen Pages of Coloured Plates in each Vol. Crown 4to. Each.

Bible Educator, The. Edited by the Very Rev. Dean Plumptre, D.D. Illustrated. Complete in Four Vols. Cloth, each. (*Also in Two Vols.,* 21s. *or* 24s.)

Co-operation in Land Tillage. By M. A.

Ladies' Physician, The. By a London Physician.

6/6

Work. An Illustrated Journal of Practice and Theory for all Workmen, Professional and Amateur. Volume IV.

EDUCATIONAL.

7/6

Modern Europe, A History of. By C. A. Fyffe, M.A., late Fellow of University College, Oxford. *Popular Illustrated Edition.* Complete in Three Vols. Each.

Practical Electricity. By Prof. W. E. Ayrton. Illustrated.

Figure Painting in Water-Colours. With Sixteen Coloured Plates. With Instructions by the Artists.

English Literature, A First Sketch of. By Prof. Henry Morley. *Revised and Enlarged Edition.*

Algebra, Manual of. By Galbraith and Haughton.

English Literature, Library of. By Professor Henry Morley. With Illustrations taken from Original MSS. *Popular Edition.* Vol. I.: SHORTER ENGLISH POEMS. Vol. 2.: ILLUSTRATIONS OF ENGLISH RELIGION. Vol. III.: ENGLISH PLAYS. Vol. IV.: SHORTER WORKS IN ENGLISH PROSE. Vol. V.: SKETCHES OF LONGER WORKS IN ENGLISH VERSE AND PROSE. Each. (*See also* £5 5s.)

Doré's Dante's Purgatory and Paradise. Illustrated by Gustave Doré. *Cheap Edition.*

Doré's Dante's Inferno. Illustrated by Gustave Doré, with Introduction by A. J. Butler. *Popular Edition.* Cloth gilt, or in buckram.

Physiology for Students, Elementary. By Alfred T. Schofield, M.D., M.R.C.S. With Two Coloured Plates and numerous Illustrations.

Chums. The Illustrated Paper for Boys. First Yearly Volume.

The Home Life of the Ancient Greeks. Translated from the German by Alice Zimmern. With Numerous Illustrations.

The Story of Africa and its Explorers. By Dr. Robert Brown, F.L.S. Illustrated. Vols I. and II. Each.

Football, The Rugby Union Game. Edited by Rev. F. Marshall. Illustrated.

Smuggling Days and Smuggling Ways; or, The Story of a Lost Art. By Commander the Hon. Henry N. Shore, R.N. With numerous Plans and Drawings by the Author.

Life and Letters of the Rt. Hon. Sir Joseph Napier, Bart., LL.D., &c., Ex-Lord Chancellor of Ireland. By Alex. Charles Ewald, F.S.A. *New and Revised Edition.*

Robinson Crusoe, Cassell's New Fine-Art Edition of. With upwards of 100 Original Illustrations by Walter Paget. Cloth gilt, gilt edges, or in buckram.

Heroes of Britain in Peace and War. With 300 Illustrations. Two Vols. in One. (*See also* 3s. 6d.)

Disraeli in Outline. By F. Carroll Brewster, LL.D.

The Journal of Marie Bashkirtseff. Translated by Mathilde Blind. With Two Portraits and an Autograph Letter. *Popular Edition in One Vol.*

Letters of Marie Bashkirtseff. Translated by Mary J. Serrano, with Portrait, Autograph Letters, Sketches, &c.

The History Scrap Book. With nearly 1,000 Engravings. *Cloth gilt, gilt edges.*

Hygiene and Public Health. By B. Arthur Whitelegge, M.D. Illustrated. *New and Revised Edition.*

Climate and Health Resorts. By Dr. Burney Yeo.

Health at School. By Clement Dukes, M.D., B.S.

The Chess Problem ; Text-Book with Illustrations. Containing 400 Positions selected from the Works of C. Planck and others.

Medical Handbook of Life Assurance. By J. E. Pollock, M.D., and J. Chisholm.

Domestic Dictionary, Cassell's. Illustrated. 1,280 pages. Royal 8vo, cloth. (*Also in roxburgh,* 10s. 6d.)

Subjects of Social Welfare. By the Rt. Hon. Lord Playfair, K.C.B.

Saturday Journal, Cassell's. Yearly Volume. Illustrated.

Cities of the World. Illustrated throughout with fine Illustrations and Portraits. Complete in Four Vols. Each.

Peoples of the World, The. By Dr. Robert Brown. Illustrated. Six Vols. Each.

Countries of the World, The. By Robert Brown, M.A., Ph.D., F.L.S., F.R.G.S. Complete in Six Vols., with 750 Illustrations. Each. (*Library binding,* 37s. 6d.)

Cassell's Concise Cyclopædia. With 600 Illustrations. A Cyclopædia in One Volume. *New and Cheap Edition.*

Cassell's New Biographical Dictionary, containing Memoirs of the most Eminent Men and Women of all Ages and Countries.

7/6 cont'd.

Year-Book of Treatment, The. A Critical Review for Practitioners of Medicine. Tenth year of publication.

Our Own Country. Complete in Six Vols. With 200 Original Illustrations in each Vol. Each. (*see also* 37s. 6d.)

English Literature, Dictionary of. By W. Davenport Adams. Cloth. (*Also in roxburgh,* 10s. 6d.)

Sea, The: its Stirring Story of Adventure, Peril, and Heroism. By F. Whymper. Four Vols., with 400 Original Illustrations. Each.

Work. Yearly Vols. II. and III.

World of Wonders, The. Two Vols. Illustrated. Each.

World of Wit and Humour, The. With about 400 Illustrations.

Natural History, Cassell's Concise. By Prof. E. Perceval Wright, M.A. Illustrated. Cloth. (*Also kept half bound.*)

RELIGIOUS.

"Quiver" Volume, The. *New and Enlarged Series.* With several hundred Contributions. About 600 Original Illustrations. Cloth.

Farrar's Life of Christ. *Cheap Illustrated Edition.* Large 4to, Cloth. (*See also* 10s. 6d.) *Popular Edition.* (*See also* 6s., 10s. 6d., 15s., 24s., *and* 42s.)

Farrar's Early Days of Christianity. *Popular Edition.* Cloth, gilt edges. (*See also* 6s., 10s. 6d., 15s., 24s., *and* 42s.)

Farrar's Life and Work of St. Paul. *Popular Edition.* Cloth, gilt edges. (*See also* 6s., 10s. 6d., 15s., 21s., 24s., *and* 42s.)

"Sunday": its Origin, History, and Present Obligation (Bampton Lectures, 1860). By the Ven. Archdeacon Hessey, D.C.L. *Fifth Edition.*

Child's Life of Christ, The. With about 200 Original Illustrations. Cloth. (*Also at* 10s. 6d., *and Demy 4to Edition,* 21s.)

Child's Bible. *Cheap Edition.* Illustrated. Cloth. *Also a superior edition at* 10s. 6d.

8/6

Moses and Geology; or, The Harmony of the Bible with Science. By the Rev. Samuel Kinns, Ph.D., F.R.A.S. With 110 Illustrations. (*New Edition on larger and superior paper.*)

9/-

Old and New Paris. A Narrative of its History, its People, and its Places. By H. Sutherland Edwards. Profusely Illustrated. Vol. I. (*Also in gilt edges,* 10s. 6d.)

The World of Romance. Illustrated. Cloth.

Conquests of the Cross. Edited by Edwin Hodder. Illustrated. Complete in Three Vols. Each.

Adventure, The World of. Complete in Three Vols. Fully Illustrated. Each.

Queen Victoria, The Life and Times of. Complete in Two Vols. Illustrated. Each.

Our Earth and its Story. By Dr. Robert Brown, F.L.S. Complete in 3 Vols. With Coloured Plates and numerous Wood Engravings. Each.

Gleanings from Popular Authors. Complete in Two Vols. With Original Illustrations by the best artists. Each. (*Also in One Vol.,* 15s.)

Natural History, Cassell's New. Edited by Prof. P. Martin Duncan, M.D., F.R.S. Complete in Six Vols. Illustrated throughout. Extra crown 4to. Each.

Universal History, Cassell's Illustrated. Vol. I., Early and Greek History. Vol. II., The Roman Period. Vol. III., The Middle Ages. Vol. IV., Modern History. With Illustrations. Each.

England, Cassell's Illustrated History of. With about 2,000 Illustrations. Complete in Ten Vols. Each. *New and Revised Edition.* Vols. I. to VI. Each. (*See also* £5.)

Protestantism, The History of. By the Rev. J. A. Wylie, LL.D. Three Vols. With 600 Illustrations. Each. (*See also* 30s.)

United States, History of the (Cassell's). Complete in Three Vols. About 600 Illustrations. Each. (*Library Edition,* 30s.)

"Family Magazine" Volume, Cassell's. With about 400 Original Illustrations.

British Battles on Land and Sea. Three Vols. With about 600 Engravings. Each. (*See also* 30s.)

Battles, Recent British. Illustrated. (*Also in imitation roxburgh,* 10s.)

Russo-Turkish War, Cassell's History of. With about 500 Illustrations. Two Vols. Each. (*See also* 15s.)

India, Cassell's History of. By James Grant. Illustrated. Two Vols. Each. (*Also Library Edition, Two Vols. in One,* 15s.)

London, Old and New. Complete in Six Vols. Containing about 1,200 Illustrations. Each. (*See also* £3.)

Edinburgh, Cassell's Old and New. Complete in Three Vols. With 600 Original Illustrations. Each. (*See also* 27s. *and* 30s.)

London, Greater. Complete in Two Vols. By Edward Walford. With about 400 Original Illustrations. Each. (*See also* 20s.)

Science for All. *Revised Edition.* Complete in Five Vols. Each containing about 350 Illustrations and Diagrams. Each.

10/-

School Registers. (*For description, see* 1s. 4d.)

10/6

Old Dorset, Chapters in the History of the County. By H. J. Moule, M.A.

The Doré Don Quixote. With about 400 Illustrations by Gustave Doré. *Cheap Edition.*

With Thackeray in America. By Eyre Crowe, A.R.A. With upwards of One Hundred Illustrations.

The Highway of Letters, and Its Echoes of Famous Footsteps. By Thomas Archer. Illustrated.

Agrarian Tenures. By the Rt. Hon. G. Shaw-Lefevre, M.P.

Historic Houses of the United Kingdom. Illustrated. Cloth gilt.

The Career of Columbus. By Charles Elton, F.S.A.

Modern Odyssey, The ; or, Ulysses up to Date. By Wyndham F. Tufnell. A Book of Travels. Illustrated.

Watts Phillips. Author and Playwright. By E. Watts Phillips. With 2 Plates.

Richard Redgrave, C.B., R.A. Memoir. Compiled from his Diary. With Portrait and Three Illustrations. By F. M. Redgrave.

Celebrities of the Century. Being a Dictionary of the Men and Women of the Nineteenth Century. Edited by Lloyd C. Sanders. *Cheap Edition.* Cloth.

Dictionary of Religion, The. By the Rev. William Benham, B.D. *Cheap Edition.* Cloth.

Farrar's Life of Christ. *Cheap Illustrated Edition.* (*See also* 7s. 6d.) *Popular Edition.* Persian morocco. (*See also* 6s., 7s. 6d., 15s., 24s., *and* 42s.)

10/6 cont'd.

Electricity in the Service of Man. A Popular and Practical Treatise. With nearly 850 Illustrations. *New and Revised Edition.*

Farrar's Life and Work of St. Paul. *Popular Edition.* Persian morocco. (*See also* 6s., 7s. 6d., 15s., 21s., 24s., *and* 42s.)

Farrar's Early Days of Christianity. *Popular Edition.* Persian morocco. (*See also* 6s., 7s. 6d., 15s., 24s., *and* 42s.)

Building Construction Plates. A series of 40 drawings. Cloth. (Or Copies of any plate may be obtained in quantities of not less than one dozen, price 1s. 6d. per dozen.)

The Polytechnic Technical Scales. On celluloid (in case). Per set. (*See also* 1s.)

Architectural Drawing. By R. Phené Spiers. Illustrated.

Encyclopædic Dictionary, The. A New and Original Work of Reference to the Words in the English Language. Complete in Fourteen Divisional Vols. Each. (*See also* 21s. *and* 25s.)

English History, The Dictionary of. *Cheap Edition.* Cloth. (*Also in roxburgh,* 15s.)

Arabian Nights' Entertainments, The. With Illustrations by Gustave Doré, and other well-known Artists. *New Edition.*

Poultry, The Book of. By Lewis Wright. *Popular Edition.* With Illustrations on Wood. (*See also* 31s. 6d. *and* £2 2s.)

Gun and its Development, The. With Notes on Shooting. By W. W. Greener. With Illustrations.

12/-

Henriette Ronner. The Painter of Cat-Life and Cat-Character. Containing a Series of Beautiful Illustrations. *Popular 4to Edition.* (*See also* 50s.)

Cassell's Miniature Shakespeare. Complete in 12 Vols. In Box. (*See also* 1s., 21s., *and* 52s. 6d.)

12/6

British Railways. Their Passenger Services, Rolling Stock, Locomotives, Gradients, and Express Speeds. By J. Pearson Pattison. With Numerous Plates.

American Life. By Paul de Rousiers. Translated from the French by A. J. Herbertson.

"Graven in the Rock"; or, the Historical Accuracy of the Bible Confirmed by references to the Assyrian and Egyptian Sculptures in the British Museum and elsewhere. By Rev. Dr. Samuel Kinns, F.R.A.S., &c. &c. With Numerous Illustrations.

Familiar Trees. Complete in Two Series. Forty Coloured Plates in each. Cloth gilt, or morocco. Each.

Garden Flowers, Familiar. Complete in Five Series. Forty Coloured Plates in each. Cloth gilt, or morocco. Each.

Wild Birds, Familiar. Complete in Four Series. By W. Swaysland. With Forty Full-page exquisite Coloured Illustrations. Cloth gilt, in cardboard box, or morocco, cloth sides. Each.

Wild Flowers, Familiar. Complete in Five Series. By F. E. Hulme, F.L.S., F.S.A. With Forty Full-page Coloured Plates in each, and Descriptive Text. Cloth gilt, or morocco. Each.

Heavens, The Story of the. By Sir R. Stawell Ball, LL.D., F.R.S., F.R.A.S., Royal Astronomer of Ireland; Loundean Professor of Astronomy and Geometry in the University of Cambridge. *Popular Edition.* Illustrated by Chromo Plates and Wood Engravings. Also in half-morocco. (*Price on application.*)

15/-

The Cabinet Portrait Gallery. First, Second, Third, and Fourth Series. Each Containing 36 Cabinet Photographs of Eminent Men and Women. With Biographical Sketches. Each.

Horse, The Book of the. By Samuel Sidney. Thoroughly Revised and brought up to date by James Sinclair and W. C. A. Blew. With 17 Full-Page Collotype Plates of Celebrated Horses of the Day, and numerous other Illustrations. Cloth.

Social England. A Record of the Progress of the People in Religion, Laws, Learning, Arts, Science, Literature, and Manners, from the Earliest Times to the Present Day. By various writers. Edited by H. D. Traill, D.C.L. Vol. I.—From the Earliest Times to the Accession of Edward the First.

The Doré Bible. With 200 Full-page Illustrations by Gustave Doré. (*Also in leather binding, price on application.*)

Farrar's Life of Christ. *Popular Edition.* Tree-calf. (*See also* 6s., 7s. 6d., 10s. 6d., 24s., *and* 42s.)

Farrar's Life and Work of St. Paul. *Popular Edition.* Tree-calf. (*See also* 6s., 7s. 6d., 10s. 6d., 21s., 24s., *and* 42s.)

Farrar's Early Days of Christianity. *Popular Edition.* Tree-calf. (*See also* 6s., 7s. 6d., 10s. 6d., 24s., *and* 42s.)

Shakspere, The Royal. Complete in Three Vols. With Steel Plates and Wood Engravings. Each.

British Ballads. With Several Hundred Original Illustrations. Complete in Two Vols. Cloth.

Russo-Turkish War, Cassell's History of the. Illustrated. Library Binding in One Vol. (*See also* 9s.)

16/-

Longfellow's Poetical Works. Illustrated throughout. *Popular Edition.* Extra crown 4to, cloth gilt.

Rivers of Great Britain. Descriptive, Historical, Pictorial. **The Royal River: The Thames from Source to Sea.** With Several Hundred Original Illustrations. *Popular Edition.* (*See also* 42s.)

Rivers of the East Coast. With numerous highly finished Engravings. *Popular Edition.* (*See also* 42s.)

Magazine of Art, The. Yearly Vol. With 12 Etchings, Photogravures, &c., and Several Hundred Engravings.

18/-

English Sanitary Institutions. By Sir John Simon, K.C.B., F.R.S., formerly the Medical Officer of Her Majesty's Privy Council.

Picturesque Europe. *Popular Edition.* Complete in Five Vols. With Thirteen exquisite Steel Plates, and numerous original Wood Engravings. Each. (*See also* 31s. 6d., £21, £31 10s., *and* £52 10s.)

Natural History Wall Sheets. Set of Ten Subjects. Unmounted. (*See also* 2s. 6d. *and* 25s.)

21/-

Sun, The Story of the. By Sir Robert Stawell Ball, LL.D., F.R.S., F.R.A.S. Illustrated with Eight Coloured Plates.

Astronomy, The Dawn of. A Study of the Astronomy and Temple Worship of the Ancient Egyptians. By J. Norman Lockyer, F.R.S., F.R.A.S., &c. Illustrated.

Tiny Luttrell. By E. W. Hornung. (Two Vols.)

New Light on the Bible and the Holy Land. By B. T. A. Evetts, M.A. Illustrated.

A Diary of the Salisbury Parliament. By H. W. Lucy. Illustrated by Harry Furniss.

Waterloo Letters. Edited by Major-General H. T. Siborne, late Colonel R.E. With numerous Plans of the Battlefield.

Thackeray, Character Sketches from. Six New and Original Drawings by F. Barnard, reproduced in Photogravure.

21/- cont'd.

Dickens, Character Sketches from. First, Second, and Third Series. By Frederick Barnard. Each containing Six Plates printed on India paper. (In Portfolio.) Each.

Abbeys and Churches of England and Wales, The. Descriptive, Historical, Pictorial. *Fine Paper Edition.* Series II.

A Vision of Saints. By Lewis Morris. *Edition de Luxe.* With 20 Full-page Illustrations.

Encyclopædic Dictionary, The. Seven Double Divisional Vols., half-morocco. Each. (*See also* 10s. 6d. *and* 25s.)

Health, The Book of. Cloth. (*Also in roxburgh,* 25s.)

Family Physician, The. A Modern Manual of Domestic Medicine. *New and Revised Edition.* Cloth. (*Also in roxburgh,* 25s.)

Milton's Paradise Lost. Illustrated with Full-page Drawings by Gustave Doré.

Shakespeare, The Plays of. Edited by Prof. Henry Morley. Thirteen Vols., in box, cloth. (*Also half-morocco, cloth sides,* 42s.)

Shakespeare, Cassell's Miniature. Complete in 12 Vols. In box with spring catch. (*See also* 1s. *and* 12s.)

Mechanics, The Practical Dictionary of. Containing 20,000 Drawings of Machinery. Four Vols. Each. (*See also* 25s.)

RELIGIOUS WORKS.

Holy Land and the Bible, The. By the Rev. Cunningham Geikie, D.D., LL.D. Edin. *Illustrated Edition.* One Vol.

Farrar's Life and Work of St. Paul. ILLUSTRATED EDITION. (*See also* 6s., 7s. 6d., 10s. 6d., 15s., 24s. *and* 42s.)

Old Testament Commentary for English Readers, The. Edited by the Rev. C. J. Ellicott, D.D., Lord Bishop of Gloucester and Bristol. Five Vols. Each. (*See also* £7 17s. 6d.)

New Testament Commentary. Edited by C. J. Ellicott, D.D., Lord Bishop of Gloucester and Bristol. Three Vols. Each. (*See also* £4 14s. 6d.)

24/-

Holy Land and the Bible, The. By the Rev. Cunningham Geikie, D.D., LL.D. Edin. With Map. In Two Vols.

Early Days of Christianity, The. By the Ven. Archdeacon Farrar, D.D., F.R.S. *Library Edition.* Two Vols., demy 8vo. (*See also* 6s., 7s. 6d., 10s. 6d., 15s., *and* 42s.)

Life of Christ, The. By the Ven. Archdeacon Farrar, D.D., F.R.S. *Library Edition.* Two Vols., cloth. (*See also* 6s., 7s. 6d., 10s. 6d., 15s., *and* 42s.)

Farrar's Life and Work of St. Paul. *Library Edition.* Two Vols., cloth. (*See also* 6s., 7s. 6d., 10s. 6d., 15s., 21s., *and* 42s.)

Our Railways, Their Development, Enterprise, Incident, and Romance. By John Pendleton. Two Vols. Illustrated, demy 8vo.

25/-

British Empire Map of the World. New Map for Schools and Institute. By G. R. Parkin and J. G. Bartholomew, F.R.G.S. Mounted on Cloth, varnished, and with Rollers.

Natural History Wall Sheets. Set of Ten Subjects. Mounted on rollers and varnished. (*See also* 2s. 6d. *and* 20s.)

Household, Cassell's Book of the. With numerous Illustrations. Four Vols. in Two, half-morocco. (*See also* 5s.)

Cathedrals, Abbeys, and Churches of England and Wales. Descriptive, Historical, Pictorial. Cloth gilt, gilt edges. *Popular Edition.* Two Vols.

Encyclopædic Dictionary, The. Seven Double Divisional Vols., half-russia. Each. (*See also* 10s. 6d. *and* 21s.)

Mechanics, The Practical Dictionary of. Half-morocco. Four Vols. Each. (*See also* 21s.)

London, Greater. *Library Edition.* Two Vols. (*See also* 9s.)

27/-

Protestantism, The History of. By the Rev. J. A. Wylie, LL.D. Containing upwards of 600 Original Illustrations. Three Vols. (*See also* 9s. *and* 30s.)

British Battles on Land and Sea. Three Vols. Cloth. (*See also* 9s. *and* 30s.)

Edinburgh, Old and New. Complete in Three Vols. (*See also* 9s. *and* 30s.)

30/-

The Universal Atlas. A New and Complete General Atlas of the World, with 117 Pages of Maps, handsomely produced in Colours, and a Complete Index to about 125,000 Names. Cloth. Net. Also half-morocco, 35s. net.

Edinburgh, Old and New. Complete in Three Vols., library binding. (*See also* 9s. *and* 27s.)

Protestantism, The History of. *Library Edition.* (*See also* 9s. *and* 27s.)

British Battles on Land and Sea. With about 600 Illustrations. *Library Edition.* Three Vols. (*See also* 9s. *and* 27s.)

31/6

Planet, The Story of Our. By T. G. Bonney, D.Sc., LL.D., F.R.S., F.S.A., F.G.S. With Six Coloured Plates and Maps and about 100 Illustrations.

List, ye Landsmen! A Romance of Incident. By W. Clark Russell. Three Volumes.

The Lake Dwellings of Europe. By Robert Munro, M.D., M.A. Illustrated. Cloth. (*Also in roxburgh,* £2 2s.)

Music, Illustrated History of. By Emil Naumann. Edited by the Rev. Sir F. A. Gore Ouseley, Bart. Illustrated. Two Vols.

Picturesque Europe. *Popular Edition.* Two Vols. in One, forming the British Isles. (*See also* 18s., £21, £31 10s., *and* £52 10s.)

Poultry, The Illustrated Book of. By Lewis Wright. *New and Revised Edition.* With Fifty Coloured Plates. Cloth gilt. (*See also* 10s. 6d. *and* 42s.)

Pigeons, The Book of. By Robert Fulton. Edited and arranged by Lewis Wright. With Fifty life-like Coloured Plates. (*Also in half-morocco,* 42s.)

32/-

The Diplomatic Reminiscences of Lord Augustus Loftus, P.C., G.C.B. First and Second Series, each in two vols. Each.

The Life, Letters, and Friendships of Richard Monckton Milnes, First Lord Houghton. By T. Wemyss Reid. Two Vols., with Two Portraits.

35/-

Butterflies and Moths, European. By W. F. Kirby. With Sixty-one life-like Coloured Plates.

Dog, Illustrated Book of the. By Vero Shaw, B.A. Cantab. With Twenty-eight Fac-simile Coloured Plates. Demy 4to, cloth gilt. (*See also* 45s.)

Canaries and Cage-Birds, The Illustrated Book of. With Fifty-six Fac-simile Coloured Plates, and numerous Wood Engravings. (*Also in half-morocco,* 45s.)

37/6   **Our Own Country.** Three Vols. *Library Binding.* (*For description, see* 7s. 6d.)

42/-   **The Picturesque Mediterranean.** Magnificently Illustrated. Coloured Frontispiece by Birket Foster. Complete in Two Vols. Each.

Rivers of Great Britain. Descriptive, Historical, Pictorial. **The Royal River: The Thames from Source to Sea.** With Several Hundred Original Illustrations. *Original Edition.* (*See also* 16s.)

Rivers of the East Coast. With numerous highly-finished Engravings. Royal 4to, with Etching as Frontispiece. (*See also* 16s.)

Doré Gallery, The. *Popular Edition.* With 250 Illustrations by Gustave Doré. Cloth gilt, bevelled boards.

Egypt: Descriptive, Historical, and Picturesque. *Popular Edition.* By Prof. G. Ebers. Translated by Clara Bell, with Notes by Samuel Birch, LL.D., D.C.L., F.S.A. 2 Vols. With about 800 Original Engravings.

Picturesque America. Complete in Four Vols., with Forty-eight Exquisite Steel Plates and about 800 Original Wood Engravings. Each.

The Life of Christ. By the Ven. Archdeacon Farrar, D.D. *Library Edition*, morocco. Two Vols. (*See also* 6s., 7s. 6d., 10s. 6d., 15s., *and* 24s.)

St. Paul, The Life and Work of. By the Ven. Archdeacon Farrar. *Library Edition*, morocco. *Illustrated Edition*, morocco. (*See also* 6s., 7s. 6d., 10s. 6d., 15s., 21s., *and* 24s.)

Farrar's Early Days of Christianity. *Library Edition.* Two Vols. Morocco. (*See also* 6s., 7s. 6d., 10s. 6d., 15s., *and* 24s.)

Poultry, The Book of. By Lewis Wright. With Fifty Coloured Plates, half-morocco. (*See also* 10s. 6d. *and* 31s. 6d.)

45/-   **Horse, The Book of the.** By Samuel Sidney. With Twenty-eight Fac-simile Coloured Plates. Half-morocco.

Dog, Illustrated Book of the. By Vero Shaw, B.A. With Twenty-eight Coloured Plates. Half-morocco. (*See also* 35s.)

50/-   **Popular Educator, Cassell's New.** With New Text, New Illustrations, New Coloured Plates, New Maps in Colours, New Size, New Type. Complete. Eight Vols. in Four, half-morocco. (*See also* 5s.)

Bible, Cassell's Illustrated Family. *Toned Paper Edition.* Leather, gilt edges. (*See also* 70s. *and* 75s.)

50/- *cont'd.*

Henriette Ronner. The Painter of Cat-Life and Cat-Character. With Portrait and 12 full-page Illustrations in Photogravure and 16 Typogravures. The Text by M. H. Spielmann. *Quarto Edition*, with Photogravures on India paper. (*See also* 12s.)

60/-   **London, Old and New.** *Complete in Six Vols.* With about 1,200 Illustrations. *Library Edition.* (*See also* 9s.)

63/-   **Shakespeare, Royal Quarto.** Edited by Charles and Mary Cowden Clarke, and containing about 600 Illustrations by H. C. Selous. Three Vols., cloth gilt.

70/-   **Bible, Cassell's Illustrated Family.** Morocco antique. (*Also* 50s. *in leather, and* 75s. *best morocco.*)

The International Shakspere. *Edition de Luxe.* "King Henry VIII." Illustrated by Sir James Linton, P.R.I. (*Limited Edition. Price on application*). "Othello." Illustrated by Frank Dicksee, R.A. "King Henry IV." Illustrated by Herr Eduard Grützner. "As You Like It." Illustrated by the late Mons. Emile Bayard. "Romeo and Juliet" advanced to £7 10s. (Now out of print.)

£4/14/6   **New Testament Commentary, The.** Edited by Bishop Ellicott. Three Vols. in half-morocco. (*See also* 21s.)

£5   **England, Cassell's History of.** With 2,000 Illustrations. *Library Edition.* Ten Vols. (*See also* 9s.)

£5/5   **English Literature, Library of.** The Set of Five Vols., half-morocco. (*See also* 7s. 6d.)

£6/6   **Picturesque Canada.** A Delineation by Pen and Pencil of all the Features of Interest in the Dominion of Canada, from its Discovery to the Present Day. With about 600 Original Illustrations. Complete in Two Volumes. The Set.

£7/17/6   **Old Testament Commentary, The.** Edited by Bishop Ellicott. Five Vols. in half-morocco. (*See also* 21s.)

£12/12   **British Fossil Reptiles, A History of.** By Sir Richard Owen, K.C.B., F.R.S., &c. With 268 Plates. Complete in Four Volumes.

£15   **Holy Bible, The.** Illustrated by Gustave Doré. Two Vols., best polished morocco.

£21   **Picturesque Europe.** *Large Paper Edition.* Complete in Five Volumes. Each containing Thirteen exquisite Steel Plates, from Original Drawings, and nearly 200 Original Illustrations, with descriptive Letterpress. Royal 4to, cloth gilt, £21; half-morocco, £37 10s.; morocco gilt, £52 10s. (*See also* 18s. *and* 31s. 6d.)

MONTHLY SERIAL PUBLICATIONS.

Art, Magazine of. With Three Plates. **1s. 4d.**
Africa, The Story of. 7d.
Biblewomen and Nurses. 2d.
British Ballads. 7d.
British Battles on Land and Sea. 7d.
Bunyan, Cassell's Illustrated. 3d.
Cabinet Portrait Gallery, The. 1s.
Canaries and Cage-Birds. 6d.
Cassell's Magazine. 7d.
Cassell's Natural History. *New Edition.* 7d.
Cassell's Penny Illustrated Stories. 1d.
Child's Bible and Child's Life of Christ. 3d.
Chums. The Illustrated Paper for Boys. **6d.**
Cottage Gardening. 3d.
Doré Don Quixote, The. 3d.
Doré Gallery, The. 7d.

Electricity in the Service of Man. 6d.
Encyclopædic Dictionary. 1s.
England, History of. 7d.
Family Physician, The. 7d.
Football. 6d.
Franco-German War. 7d.
Gardening, Cassell's Popular. 7d.
Gazetteer, Cassell's. 7d.
Health, Book of. 6d.
Horse, Book of the. 7d.
Household, Book of the. 7d.
Little Folks. 6d.
London, Greater. 7d.
New Testament Commentary, The. Edited by BISHOP ELLICOTT. 7d.
Our Earth and its Story. 7d.
Our Own Country. 7d.
Paris, Old and New. 7d.
Peoples of the World. 7d.
Picturesque America. 1s.

Picturesque Europe. 1s.
Pigeons, Fulton's Book of. 6d.
Quiver, The. 6d.
Saturday Journal, Cassell's. 6d.
Science for All. 7d.
Shakspere, The Royal. 7d.
Storehouse of General Information, Cassell's. 7d.
Sunday School Teacher's Bible Manual. 6d.
Sunshine Series, Cassell's. 1s.
Surgery, Annals of. 2s.
Technical Educator, New. 6d.
Trees, Familiar. 6d.
Universal History. 7d.
Wild Flowers, Familiar. 6d.
Work. 6d.

Cassell's Railway Time Tables and Through-Route Glance-Guide. *Enlarged Series.* Price 4d.

WEEKLY PUBLICATIONS.

Chums. 1d.
Cottage Gardening. ½d.

Doré Don Quixote. ½d.
National Library, Cassell's. Paper, **3d.** ; Cloth, **6d.**

Saturday Journal, Cassell's. 1d.
Work. 1d.

Letts's Diaries and other Time-Saving Publications are published exclusively by CASSELL & COMPANY, and particulars will be forwarded post free on application to the Publishers,

CASSELL & COMPANY, Limited, *Ludgate Hill, London; Paris and Melbourne.*

9 782019 953577